Chesapeake ABC

by Priscilla Cummings
illustrated by David Aiken

Published by Schiffer Publishing Ltd. 2011
Chesapeake ABC was originally published by
Tidewater Publishers in 2000.

A is for an anchor,
So heavy it will stay
Wherever it is dropped
So a ship won't drift away.

B is for a boat.
B also stands for Bay.
Boating on the Bay—
What a perfect summer day!

C is for a crab,
For its claw and for a creek.
You'll find them in the Bay
We call the Chesapeake.

D is for a dock,
A walkway on the water.
You can tie a boat there,
Or fish, or see an otter!

E is for the egret,
So feathery and fair.
E also stands for eel,
Who slithers here and there.

F is for the flounder,
A fish that's flat and wide
And F is for a frog,
Who likes to hop and hide.

G is for the geese
Who fly in flocks in fall.
G also stands for gosling,
The smallest goose of all.

H is for a heron,
A bird known for its height.
Great blue they call this heron.
Its bill is quite a sight!

I is for the Indians
Who gave the Bay its name.
Indians lived here long ago,
Before explorers came.

J is for the jellies—
That's jellyfish we mean.
Blobbing, bobbing jellyfish,
The most you've ever seen!

K is for a kayak,
A kind of boat that's low.
Explore the Bay by kayak.
Take time and paddle slow.

L is for a lighthouse.
There are many in the Bay.
At night each shines a light
So boats can see the way.

M is for the marsh
And for a muskrat, too.
Muskrats in the marsh—
Can you spot more than two?

N is for a net.
There are two kinds to use.
A fish net or a crab net,
It's up to you to choose.

O is for the oysters
Who lie in crusty layers.
And O is for the Orioles,
Some birds and baseball players.

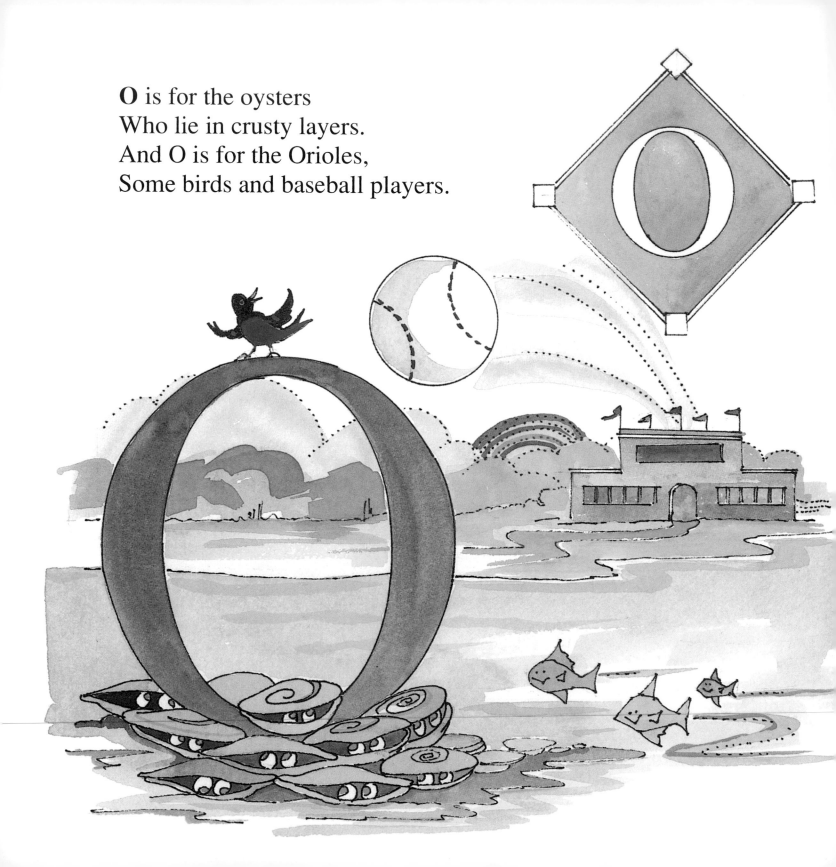

P is for a port,
Boats moving all about.
Cargo ships go in to port,
Unload, and then go out.

Q is for quack, quack!
That's how ducks like to talk.
"Quack, quack! Let's go in swimming!"
"Quack, quack! Let's take a walk!"

R is for the rockfish
And for retriever, too.
The Chesapeake retriever
Will fetch all day for you!

S is for a seagull,
For sand and swim and sun.
Lots of people travel
To the Bay to have some fun!

T stands for a turtle.
See this one in the flowers?
It found a sunny spot
And wants to nap for hours.

U is for underwater.
Underwater in the Bay
A whole wide world of creatures
Lives each and every day.

V is for a vulture,
A big, black bird you'll see
Flying high in circles
Or sitting in a tree.

W is for water,
For wind and for a wave.
Sometimes sailors sailing
Must be very brave.

X is for extra special
And that's the Bay to me!
Few words start with X alone
So here it blends with E.

Y is for a yacht,
A fine and fancy boat.
Some yachts are so gigantic
It's a wonder they can float!

Z is for a zephyr,
A soft and gentle breeze,
Blowing small white sails
And moving boats with ease.

Now you know your ABCs,
With C for crab and creek.
If you've never seen the Bay
Please come and take a peek!